Great Mysteries
BIGFOOT

by Ruth Shannon Odor
illustrated by Diana Magnuson

D1569478

Created by

THE
CHILD'S
WORLD

MANKATO, MN 56001

cover photograph / copyright Rene Dahinden
cover design by Kathryn Schoenick

Library of Congress Cataloging-in-Publication Data

Odor, Ruth Shannon, 1926-
  Bigfoot / by Ruth Shannon Odor ; illustrated by Diana L. Magnuson.
    p. cm. — (Great mysteries)
  Includes index.
  Summary: Examines the history of sightings of the mysterious hairy
creature known as Bigfoot and discusses possible explanations.
  ISBN 0-89565-455-5 -1991 Edition
    1. Sasquatch—Juvenile literature.   [1. Sasquatch.]
I. Magnuson, Diana, ill.   II. Title.   III. Series: Great mysteries
(Elgin, Ill.)
QL89.2.S2036   1989
001.9′44—dc19   88-7882
                                                        CIP
                                                        AC

©1989 The Child's World, Inc.

Great Mysteries

BIGFOOT

CONTENTS

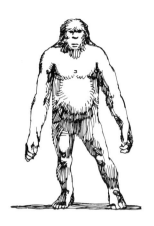

Chapter 1

What is Bigfoot?

You and your family are hiking through a forest. Shh! What is that sound? It's water rushing over the rocks in a mountain stream. You leave the trail for a few minutes to see the rushing water. Small, smooth, white stones lie beside the stream. You bend over to pick up a few. As you raise your head, you see a huge, dark shape beside some tall trees on the opposite bank.

It's a man! No, it's much taller than a man. And it's covered with hair. It's a bear! No, it's standing easily on *two* feet.

A cold chill runs up and down your spine, and you can feel the hair stand up on the back of your neck. You stand frozen, unable to move, but the huge creature just turns and walks off into the forest. Soon the tall trees hide it from view. Could it be that you have just seen one of the mysterious creatures known as Bigfoot?

An Unsolved Riddle

The mystery of Bigfoot is one of the great unsolved riddles of all time. Are there really huge creatures, part animal and part human, who stalk the uninhabited areas of the world, leaving behind huge footprints? Some sightings are just imagination. And some of them are just fakes. But are all of them one or the other? How can we be sure that not one of these sightings is real?

Monsters in History

People have always told stories about monsters and giants and other strange creatures. Tales about animals that act like humans are especially popular. Some of these stories are just made-up stories, meant to scare people or entertain children. Others are thought to be true. People have been telling stories about Bigfoot-like creatures for a long time.

Ancient stories of the Norsemen tell of Leif Eriksson and his men sailing across the ocean to the New World (North America) a thousand years ago. When they came ashore, according to the legend, they met horrible, hairy, ugly creatures with great black eyes. The creatures seemed more human than animal, but they couldn't have been Indians because Indians don't look hairy—especially to a Viking! Could this possibly have been the first sighting of Bigfoot in North America?

For hundreds of years the Indians of the Pacific North-

west Coast have handed down stories of giant, hairy monsters that seem somehow human. The Yuroks called them *Toki-mussi*. The Hupa Indians call them *Oh-mahs*, which sounds like a good name. If you ever saw such a monster, you would probably say, "Oh! My!"—unless you were too scared to say anything at all. Actually, the word "oh-mah," in the language of the Hupas, means something like "devil."

The Salish Indians have given these creatures their most famous name, Sasquatch. This name comes from folk stories about a legendary tribe of giants. One group of Indians near Vancouver, British Columbia, believes that the Sasquatch are the descendants of two bands of giants who were almost all killed in battles long ago.

All these legends seem to refer to the same mysterious monster we call Bigfoot. The question is: are these legends based on real creatures or are they just made-up stories?

Monsters in Legend

There are a lot of made-up stories about part-animal and part-human monsters. Well over a thousand years ago, an English poet told a story about a hero named Beowulf and a Bigfoot-like monster named Grendel. However, Grendel was definitely a storybook monster. One evening the huge, hideous hulk carried off thirty warriors to eat for his dinner. Grendel terrorized people for twelve years. Then the brave Beowulf arrived in town. Beowulf battled the monster and killed him.

Even though this is just a made-up story, some of the

places and events described in the story are real. This has made some people think that the idea for Grendel might have come from a real creature.

All over the world there are stories about creatures similar to Bigfoot. In China there are legends of a great stone ape. Norse myths tell of a giant called Ymir. Ancient Greek stories tell of a whole race of giants. And Roman myths speak of almost-human creatures.

We are still making up stories of huge creatures that act like humans today. One of the most famous is the story of King Kong. King Kong was a huge gorilla who fell in love with a human woman. In the movie he did some terrible things, including terrorizing the entire city of New York. Yet, when he died at the end of the movie, the audience felt sad because he had such human emotions.

The Bigfoot reported today are not movie monsters. However, it's hard to say what they are. We can't even say for sure what they look like. But when the reported descriptions are all put together, we get a general picture of Bigfoot.

Tall, Dark, and Hairy

Just as you might guess from the name, a Bigfoot is big—seven to twelve feet tall is the usual reported height, and one person said he saw a Bigfoot that was fifteen feet tall! (That's probably three times as tall as you are.) A Bigfoot can weigh over 500 pounds—and some people have reported seeing Bigfoot that weigh as much as 800 pounds! The body is covered with hair, except on the palms, soles, and face. The hair is described as black or brown or reddish-brown and is two to four inches long. Some people have reported that the hair on Bigfoot's head is longer than on the rest of its body.

The creature has a short neck, and its shoulders are broad and powerful—over a yard wide. The arms are long and much like those of a gorilla. The ferocious face is flat, with a pug nose and a sloping forehead. Some reports say the head seems to come almost to a point at the top and that Bigfoot's eyes are a glowing red.

Big Stinker

If you don't like the smell of a skunk, you definitely won't like the smell of a Bigfoot! A Bigfoot is said to give off an odor so terrible that it makes a skunk smell good. People say it smells like a sewer or like something that's

Bigfoot hunter Rene Dahinden with a statue of Bigfoot in Willow Creek, California (copyright Rene Dahinden)

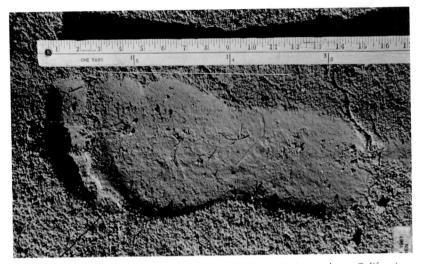

Fifteen-inch footprint found on Blue Creek Mountain in northern California, 1967 (copyright Rene Dahinden)

been dead for several days. One man said the smell was so bad it made his horse bolt.

Footprints, Not Paw Prints

The most remarkable thing about the Bigfoot is that they have human-like feet, instead of animal-like paws. This means that these creatures are like human beings, as well as like animals.

A Bigfoot walks erect, like a person. A bear can rear awkwardly onto its back legs, but it can't stride through the woods on two legs as Bigfoot has been seen to do.

Bigfoot's huge footprints measure from fifteen to twenty-two inches long and are usually about six inches wide. That's probably three times as long as your foot. The depth of Bigfoot's footprints tells us that they were made by something very heavy. One set was one inch deep in fairly hard soil. And the distance between the prints tells us that whatever made them has a very long stride.

It is because of these footprints that the Rocky Mountain Indians named this monster Bigfoot.

Behavior

The Bigfoot are thought to be intelligent, although they may be more curious than intelligent. In most cases, they seem to be more interested in watching people than in harming them. They are mostly night creatures, although they have been seen in the daytime. They are nomads, traveling here and there. And they are said to eat chiefly berries, roots, and rodents.

The cry of a Bigfoot can send chills up and down the spine. Some say it sounds like a baby crying. Others say it

"Boy, there sure are a lot of nuts in this world."

sounds like a woman screaming, or a shrill whistle or yelp. One thing is certain. It is a spooky, spine-chilling sound like no other on the face of the earth!

A Mystery

We can't really say for sure what kind of animal Bigfoot might be. We can't even say for sure that such creatures exist. Stories about creatures that look like huge apes but act human are not new. They have been around for a long, long time. The mystery is: are any of these stories based on real creatures? Read on and decide for yourself.

Chapter 2

Seeing is Believing

Down through the years, trappers, hunters, and others have told stories of having seen "wild men of the woods." The stories come from many different places at many different times. Yet, the descriptions of what people have seen remain surprisingly similar.

A Tall Thing Picking Berries

In 1886 a man named Jack Dover was hunting in the Marble Mountain area of California. He saw a huge figure picking berries from the bushes. The "thing" was seven feet tall with long hair. Its shrill voice sounded like a woman crying out in fear.

Mr. Dover aimed his gun, but the figure looked so human that he just couldn't shoot it. Several other people in the same area also claimed to have seen the "thing."

On a Snow-covered Mountain

Two Canadian brothers, who were professional prospectors, were in the wild, mountain country of British Columbia in the winter of 1965. The ground was covered with snow, and the lake was frozen. The brothers sat down to rest for a minute, leaning their backpacks against a rock. Suddenly they heard something moving among the trees about 150 yards away.

Something was standing there watching them! It was a huge, dark-colored, man-like creature. It was about eight feet tall, covered with dark brown hair, and had almost no neck. The face seemed to be hairless.

The two brothers didn't move. They watched the creature. And the creature watched them. Finally, it turned and walked away. The next day the two men found huge footprints in the snow where they had seen the strange barefoot giant.

On a Lonely Road at Midnight

One night in April of 1969, a husband and wife were driving along a lonely road through a forest in Butte County, California. Suddenly their headlights shone on a tall figure crossing the road. It looked like a man wearing a fur coat. The figure was over six feet tall and completely covered with short, black hair. Its head was small and peaked at the top. It shuffled along and turned once to look at the car.

The couple didn't think this was a man playing a trick—not at midnight on a lonely road. They didn't think it was a bear. Bears don't cross highways on their hind

legs. They could only think that it must have been a Bigfoot!

Just a Glimpse

There are thousands and thousands of stories like these, spanning at least the last hundred years. The main evidence that the Bigfoot exist is that people have seen them. Over and over again, people report brief encounters with some sort of huge, hairy creatures. A nine-year-old boy in Oregon saw one as he walked to school one morning. Two businessmen, fishing in California, saw

one as they relaxed by a peaceful stream. A woman in Utah looked out her window one night and saw one outside her house. One Bigfoot even ventured into a crowded trailer court in The Dalles, Oregon.

Only rarely is a Bigfoot encounter more than just a glimpse of a huge, hairy creature. And when people see a Bigfoot only briefly, it's easy to believe that they may have been mistaken. Perhaps it was just an ordinary animal. Or perhaps it was just some object that looked like a monster in the shadows. But sometimes people do get more than just a glimpse of Bigfoot.

Jacko, The Boy Bigfoot

One of the earliest printed reports of a Bigfoot encounter describes the actual capture of a Bigfoot.

The July 4, 1884, issue of the *Daily Colonist,* a newspaper in British Columbia, carried the story of the capture of a strange gorilla-like creature. Several sightings of such a creature had been reported by railway men. Then one day, the engineer of a train saw what he thought was a man lying asleep beside the railroad tracks. Quickly he blew the whistle to put on the brakes, and the train squealed to a stop. The "man" jumped up, barked, and climbed up the steep, rocky hill beside the tracks.

Quickly the railway men jumped from the train and chased what they thought was a crazy Indian. Finally they trapped him on a ledge and dropped a rock on his head, knocking him unconscious.

After they tied him up and took him to the station, they realized that they had not captured a crazy Indian, but rather a strange creature that was half man and half beast. They nicknamed him Jacko.

Jacko was four feet, seven inches tall and weighed 127 pounds. He looked like a man except for the fact that his entire body was covered with long black hair.

Jacko was kept in a cage and stared at like a circus animal. Finally he disappeared from the news. No one knows what happened to him. Did he die? Or escape? Was he shipped to England? Or sold to a circus?

Many people think that Jacko was a boy Bigfoot and that he had slipped and fallen from the cliff, lying beside the railroad until the noise of the train aroused him.

Whatever he was and however he came to be there, he surely caused a stir back in 1884.

A Bigfoot Picnic

A logger in Oregon got to study a Bigfoot family eating lunch. He told his story to Bigfoot investigator, John Green, but asked that his name be withheld because he didn't want people thinking he was crazy.

The logger was walking along a trail in the mountains when he saw three hairy creatures near a huge pile of rocks—a Papa Bigfoot, a Mama Bigfoot, and a Baby Bigfoot! The rocks were huge; some must have weighed as much as 100 pounds. But the two huge creatures lifted them easily, as Baby watched. They seemed to be looking for something. Then suddenly, Papa Bigfoot found a nest of rodents. They settled down to eat. Mama and Papa each ate two or three of the small creatures. Baby got one.

The logger had a long time to study the creatures, which he could see clearly. Papa Bigfoot was well over six feet tall and was covered with dark brown hair. Mama was a head shorter and a shade lighter. Baby was little, only coming up to his mother's hip. The creatures had flat, broad faces and no visible ears. They walked easily on their hind legs, as a person does.

The three creatures finished their lunch, though Baby seemed to have some trouble chewing his. Then Papa started searching again. His eyes fell upon the bushes where the logger was hidden. Papa Bigfoot gave a start and dashed off into the forest, with Mama and Baby following closely behind.

Giants at Ape Canyon

In 1924 four miners in Oregon had only a brief glimpse of a Bigfoot, but this turned into an encounter all of them wished they could forget.

A man named Fred Beck and three other men were working a mining claim in a canyon near Mount St. Helens in Washington. Occasionally they found large footprints in the sand and gravel nearby—footprints that looked like those of a large, barefoot man.

Then one day, one of the men looked up to see what appeared to be a huge ape, staring at him from behind a large rock. The man got a rifle and shot at the creature. He didn't know if he hit it or not, but the creature disappeared behind the trees and rocks.

A few days later, Fred Beck saw either the same creature or one just like it walking along a trail high above the canyon. Beck aimed and fired three shots into the creature's back. The huge creature fell into the canyon.

That night while the men were asleep in their cabin, they were awakened by a terrible noise. Thump! Thump! Thump! Rocks were hitting the roof and walls of the cabin. Several times the men went outside to see who (or what) was throwing the stones. They could find nothing. The stone-throwing stopped while they were outside, but started again as soon as they went inside.

The next night the same thing happened. And the next. This was too much! The men packed up their belongings and left.

Later a search party went into the canyon, looking for the "giant apes." They found nothing—except the little

cabin with huge rocks lying around it and the inside torn to shreds.

Evidence

Regardless of the circumstances in which a Bigfoot is seen, sightings don't prove that the Bigfoot exist. Scien-

Rene Dahinden measures a footprint found on Blue Creek Mountain, California (copyright Rene Dahinden)

tists want to see a live, captured Bigfoot, or a dead one, or even a good, clear photograph of one. No one has been able to give them such evidence. However, many people have been able to show something very real—footprints.

Barefoot in the Snow

In the year 1810 a Canadian explorer named David Thompson and his Indian guide were crossing the high, snow-covered Rocky Mountains. As they traveled up the trail, Thompson saw strange footprints in the snow. They looked like the footprints of a man who was barefoot. But they were huge. Thompson measured them and found them to be fourteen inches long and eight inches wide. No man has a foot that big!

The only creature Thompson knew of that was that big was a grizzly bear. But these were not the paw prints of a grizzly. He wondered what could have made those strange footprints in the snow. But his guide was not puzzled. He told Thompson about Bigfoot.

Imagination Doesn't Leave a Trail

A tall, hairy creature seen in the distance can be a bear, or a tree, or a practical joker. But if the thing leaves huge footprints behind, then it can't be just imagination. And if the footprints can be analyzed to prove they were made by a human-like creature that is much larger than any human being, then the footprints can be considered scientific evidence that Bigfoot exist.

Stories about the huge footprints date from the Thompson sighting and even earlier. But in more recent times the footprints have become more than just stories. Plaster casts have been made of them, photographs have been taken of them, and field studies of the actual prints have been done. Some have been shown to be fakes. But some of them can't be explained.

Bulldozing with Bigfoot

In 1958 a man named Jerry Crew was working with a road crew which was bulldozing a new road into the wilderness in Bluff Creek Valley, California. One morning when Crew went out to start his big crawler-tractor, he found footprints in the mud all around the machine. They were not prints of a boot or shoe, but of a bare, human-looking foot. And they were huge!

At first Crew thought someone was playing a joke. But who would come out into the wilderness in the middle of the night to make huge tracks? The men had neither the resources nor the energy to have pulled something like this off. The tracks came from down a nearby hill, circled the machinery, and then went down another hill and into the forest.

The crew discussed the mysterious footprints, but they couldn't come up with any explanation of them. They forgot them until a month later when the footprints appeared around the machinery again. This time Crew made plaster casts of them.

The footprints were about sixteen inches long and about eight inches wide. The average distance between prints was about fifty inches (which is almost twice as long as the step of an average person). The depth of the prints

Tracks found in Bluff Creek Valley, California (copyright Rene Dahinden)

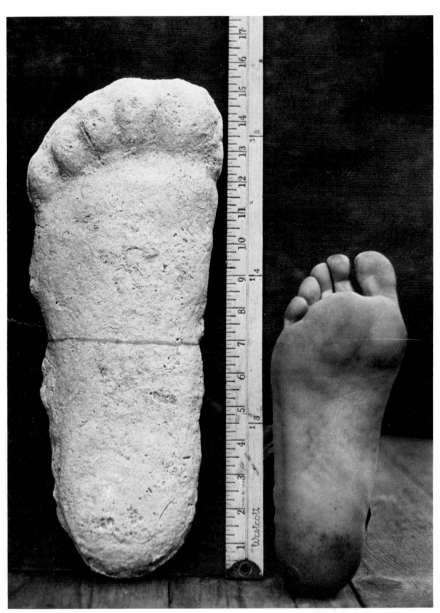

Human foot compared to cast of a Bigfoot footprint (copyright Rene Dahinden)

showed they were made by something that weighed between 750 and 800 pounds. The prints were clearly human-like, showing a heel, a ball, and five toes without noticeable claws. Whatever made them wasn't like any animal or any human known to science.

Footprints and More Footprints

Year after year people have found huge footprints—in snow, sand, earth, or mud. In 1969 near Bossburg, Washington, over a thousand footprints were found on a trail of half a mile. These seventeen-inch-long footprints were especially interesting because the creature that made them appeared to have a crippled right foot.

Most scientists dismiss the footprint evidence as unreliable. They think the footprints are just fakes. But Dr. Grover Krantz, an anthropologist, thinks that very, very few people would have the knowledge to create such appropriate prints. He analyzed footprints and casts from what he felt were reliable sources. He knew that if a print was identical to a human print, just bigger, that it would be a fake. A creature as heavy as Bigfoot would have to have some changes in its foot to carry that much weight.

When Dr. Krantz examined the footprints, he found what he was looking for. The heel was greatly enlarged compared to the rest of the foot and the ankle was set further toward the front of the foot than is a human ankle. Also, the foot had no arch and showed toes more equal in length than on a human foot. All of these things are just what a scientist would expect in a creature that weighs more than 500 pounds.

So, what is it that makes these footprints? Not bears. Their pawprints are much different. Not man. No man is that large or that heavy. Maybe it's really Bigfoot!

Bigfoot, Movie Star

Some exciting "evidence" of the existence of Bigfoot, believable to many people, came in 1967. It was a movie film of a large, female Bigfoot.

In October of 1967, Roger Patterson and Bob Gimlin, two men from the state of Washington, drove down to Bluff Creek in northern California in search of Bigfoot. One afternoon the two men were riding their horses along the dry, sandy creek bed.

As they came around a large pile of logs, they saw a female Bigfoot squatting on the bank! Suddenly, it stood up and began walking away.

The sight of this beast scared the horses so badly that Patterson's horse reared up and threw him. Patterson did manage to grab his movie camera and run after the Bigfoot. He filmed as he ran. Suddenly he was out of film—and the Bigfoot was gone.

The two men tied their horses and set out to track the Bigfoot. They couldn't find it again, but they did find its tracks in the soft sand. They made plaster casts of the footprints and then returned to civilization.

When the film was developed, it was blurry. Patterson had not had time to set the camera, and he had been running as he shot the pictures. But the film does show a large, hairy figure walking upright. The figure turned once to look at the camera and then disappeared into the trees.

Frame from the Patterson film (copyright Rene Dahinden)

"It's not real. It's just some little Bigfoot dressed in a costume."

It was about seven feet tall and weighed between 350 and 450 pounds. It had reddish-brown hair and a cone-shaped skull.

Many scientists and experts from a movie studio looked at the film. Some said, "It's a publicity stunt. It's a man in a fur suit. It's just a joke."

Others said, "It's real. It's proof that Bigfoot exist."

Was the 1967 film real? Or was it a well-planned trick? If it was a trick, it was carefully thought through down to the last detail. But we may never know for sure.

Scientific Proof

The scientific evidence that the Bigfoot exist is pretty slim. Yet it seems unlikely that so many people in so many places over so many years could all tell such similar stories, unless they were all seeing the same, real creatures. However, people, especially when they are scared, can make amazing mistakes. Light and shadow play all sorts of tricks on the eye. Footprints can be measured and analyzed—but they can also be faked. Even the 1967 film, realistic as it appears, could be an elaborate hoax. Scientists are not convinced that the Bigfoot exist, but thousands of other people are.

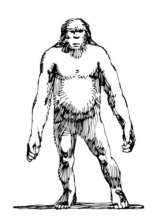

Chapter 3

Meeting Up with Bigfoot

Most people who run into Bigfoot don't stick around long enough to find out what Bigfoot is like. The sight of such a large creature is just too scary. Yet, they probably have nothing to worry about. Most reports claim Bigfoot is just a gentle giant.

The Gentle Giant

Bigfoot is often described as shy and gentle. It is said by some that this "gentle giant" peeks around trees and hides behind bushes watching people. It is curious, but not curious enough to come out into the open.

One man reported that a Bigfoot chased him. Trying to distract the creature, he pulled off his boot and threw it at the Bigfoot. The huge creature picked up the boot and sat down to look it over. On his face was a look that said, "What on earth is this?"

There have been reports of Bigfoot taking food, but leaving things in exchange. There are also stories of injured men being helped by Bigfoot.

Bigfoot, Good Samaritan

One man told of meeting a Bigfoot near his cabin in the mountains of California. The man laid down a string of fish and made a motion of friendship. The Bigfoot snatched the fish and left. Later, deerskins, wood, and wild berries were left outside the man's door. The man never knew for sure where they came from, but in the distance, he heard the cry of a Bigfoot.

Several years later that same man was attacked by a rattlesnake. The man killed the snake, but the bite made him so sick that he fainted. When he came to, he looked up to see three large Bigfoot. They had made a small cut on the snakebite, removed the venom, and covered the bite with cool moss. One Bigfoot then carried the man down the trail and left him under a tree.

I Don't Believe It

A man named William Roe worked on a Canadian highway in 1957. One day he decided to climb a nearby mountain to an old, deserted mine. He saw what he thought was a grizzly bear and sat down to watch it. When it stepped out of the bushes, he saw that it wasn't a bear at all! The thing stood on two legs. It was about six feet tall and probably weighed about 300 pounds. Its face

was flat, with a pug nose and sloping forehead, and it was covered with dark brown, silver-tipped hair.

The Bigfoot squatted down, pulled some branches to its mouth, and ate the leaves. Then it saw Roe. It looked at him in amazement. Roe said that the look was so funny he just had to grin. The creature straightened up and walked back the way it had come. It looked at Roe over its shoulder as if to say, "I don't believe it!"

Kidnapped by a Bigfoot

Bigfoot may be only curious, but sometimes that curiosity can be very frightening—especially if you're what Bigfoot is curious about!

A man named Muchalat Harry lived on Vancouver Island with his Indian tribe, the Nootkas. Muchalat Harry was known as a strong and courageous trapper. Most of the Indians wouldn't go into the forests alone. They were afraid of Bigfoot. But Muchalat Harry wasn't. Often he spent weeks all alone, trapping in the forests.

One day he traveled some distance in his canoe and then continued deep into the forest on foot. Finding a good place to camp, he built a lean-to and put out his trap line. When night came, he wrapped up in his blanket,

wearing only his long underwear, and went to sleep. In the middle of the night, he felt himself being picked up and carried away! Who (or what) could be carrying a man so easily—and so far? It was too dark to see.

Muchalat Harry was terrified! But there was nothing he could do. Finally he was dumped down on the ground. When daylight came, he saw that he was surrounded by about twenty Bigfoot of different sizes! There were males and females and children. They just stood and stared at him.

One Bigfoot came up to Muchalat Harry and touched him. The Bigfoot thought that Muchalat Harry's underwear was loose skin and pulled at it. Several others came forward and pulled at the underwear too, but they didn't hurt him.

Finally the Bigfoot got tired of looking at this strange creature and wandered off to gather food. Muchalat Harry jumped up and ran as fast as he could go! He ran downhill, past his camp, straight to his canoe. He hopped inside and began paddling as if his life depended on it—which he thought it did!

The next morning the people in his village heard someone crying out and ran down to the river. They found Muchalat Harry lying in his canoe. He was wearing only his wet, torn underwear. He was nearly frozen and completely exhausted.

Three weeks went by before Muchalat Harry was well. His hair turned white, and he said not a word. Finally, he told the story of his kidnapping. And never again did he go into the forests.

The Kidnapping of an Indian Maiden

An Indian woman living in Canada claims that she also was once kidnapped by a Bigfoot. She said that back in 1871, when she was seventeen years old, a huge man-beast captured her and made her swim with it across the river. It carried her to a rock shelter where its aged parents lived. She was scared, but the huge creatures treated her kindly. After about a year the Bigfoot took her home. When asked why, the Indian woman replied, "Because I aggravated it so much."

Prisoner of a Bigfoot Family

Canadian lumberjack, Albert Ostman, has also reported being kidnapped by a Bigfoot. He did not tell his story when it first happened because he thought no one would believe it. He didn't tell it for thirty-three years. Then, when he read so many stories about Bigfoot in the press, he came forward. Just as he expected, many people did not believe him—but many did.

Ostman reported that while on vacation in 1924, he visited the mountains of British Columbia to prospect. He found a lovely, grassy, open place to set up camp. He

Bigfoot hunter Rene Dahinden interviews Albert Ostman (copyright Rene Dahinden)

made a bed of branches and laid his sleeping bag on it. Then he hung his pack of supplies on a pole.

The next morning Ostman found that his supplies had been moved around, but that nothing was missing. Must be a porcupine, he thought.

The next morning he found his pack emptied and some of the food missing, but the salt was still there. This surprised and puzzled Ostman, for he knew that porcupines love salt. So much for the porcupine. A bear? No, if it had been a bear, he would have heard it. Who (or what) was sneaking around his camp during the night?

On the third night Ostman climbed into his sleeping bag with his clothes on. He had his boots at the bottom of

the bag and his rifle at his side. He tried to stay awake, but he couldn't. In the middle of the night, he was awakened by a strange movement. He was being picked up and carried, sleeping bag and all, like a sack of potatoes! All he could see was a huge hand holding the opening of the bag!

Thump, thump, thump. It was a long, uncomfortable trip. At times Ostman could feel himself being dragged on the ground. He felt something hard hitting against him. "Oh, it's just my pack," he thought. "There are cans of food in it."

At last he was dumped to the ground and could crawl out of the bag. Looking up, he saw four huge, hairy, almost-human creatures staring down at him! There was a father (the one that had kidnapped him), a mother, an almost-grown son, and a young daughter. Ostman stood up, looked at the four strange creatures, and asked, "What do you chaps want with me?" They didn't answer.

The father was about eight feet tall and looked as if he weighed about 550 pounds. He had long arms and large hands with short fingers. The four jabbered at one another in some speech of their own.

The Bigfoot didn't hurt Ostman, but they wouldn't let him leave. They did let him have his own place to sleep, and he could prepare his own food, using the supplies in his pack.

The Bigfoot family ate sweet grass, roots, and spruce tips from the forest. While the mother and son wandered off to find food, the father and daughter guarded their prisoner. "Do they want me for a pet?" wondered Ostman. "Or worse yet, as a husband for the daughter?"

"I must escape," he decided, and he watched for an opportunity. That opportunity came in the strangest way. The father showed interest in Ostman's box of snuff. After studying it for a long time, the Bigfoot took the snuff box and swallowed all of the snuff in it! In a few minutes, he was screaming and rolling on the ground in pain!

"Now's my chance to run away," thought Ostman. And he did.

Did Albert Ostman and the others make up their stories, or are they true? If they are true, they agree with many of the descriptions of the Bigfoot. If they aren't, they are still fun to read.

Alarming Attacks

Some people do not picture the Bigfoot as gentle giants that only bother people out of curiosity. They picture them as ferocious and dangerous monsters. There aren't a lot of reports that describe the Bigfoot this way, but there are some stories of the Bigfoot chasing hikers, destroying property, and even killing people.

One story concerns the MacLeod brothers. The MacLeod brothers were prospecting in Canada in 1910. No one suspected they were having any kind of trouble. Then one day they were found dead in a lonely valley. Their heads had been cut off. Some people of the area blamed the Bigfoot, which had been seen in the area. However, many others said that it was not fair to blame the Bigfoot when no one knew what really happened.

Another murder blamed on Bigfoot is included in Theodore Roosevelt's book *The Wilderness Hunter,* published in 1892. Roosevelt tells a story he heard from a man named Bauman. When Bauman and his partner were trapping in the mountains, they set up camp in an open area in the middle of a dark forest. While they were gone, something tore down their lean-to and scattered their belongings. It left behind huge footprints. At night they heard noises, and Bauman shot at a dark shadow. The next night they did not sleep but built a huge fire and sat beside it. Nothing appeared, but they could hear noises in the bushes. "It's time to leave this spooky place," they decided. Bauman went to check their beaver traps before they left. When he returned, he found his friend's body lying on the ground. His neck had been broken and all

"But why can't I have him for a pet?"

around were huge footprints deep in the soft soil. Bauman left everything behind and headed for home as fast as he could go!

What is Bigfoot Really Like?

These kinds of reports represent only a small number of Bigfoot sightings. Most reports of the Bigfoot describe them as aggressive only if people bother them first. If they feel threatened, they will fight back, just as any creature will. However, if treated kindly, their natural curiosity comes out. The Bigfoot still might not make very good pets, but they're really not likely to want you for dinner!

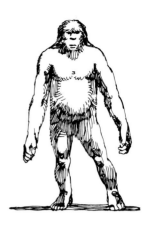

Chapter 4

The Abominable Snowman and Other Ape-men

The Bigfoot seem to be found only in North America. But all over the world creatures similar to the Bigfoot have been reported—and the resemblance seems too remarkable for coincidence.

The Yeti

The giant, forested, snowy slopes of the Himalayan Mountains are one of the most remote parts of the world. A people called the Sherpas live in those majestic mountains, which separate northern India and Tibet. For hundreds of years the Sherpas have told stories of the strange creatures they call the Yeti.

The Yeti are strange, ape-like creatures, much like Bigfoot except slightly smaller. (They're probably cousins.)

Although there is no real evidence that the Yeti exist either, again people have found large footprints and had brief glimpses of the creatures.

The Yeti are described as being half-man and half-ape. They are covered with long, fine hair, which is blonde, reddish-brown, or black. The hair is not on their faces, hands, or the soles of their feet. They have long arms that reach to their knees, and they walk on thick legs in an upright posture. They have pointed heads, flat faces, and wide mouths with large teeth. (Sound familiar?)

Abominable Snowman

The word "Yeti" is a Tibetan word meaning "dweller among the rocks." Yeti is also known as the "Abominable Snowman." That name was given by accident.

Yeti became the Abominable Snowman when Lt. Col. C. K. Howard-Bury visited the Himalayas on an expedition in 1920. Howard-Bury and his men saw some dark forms through their binoculars one afternoon. The figures were moving across the snow-covered mountain high above. When Howard-Bury and his men climbed to the spot where they had seen the figures, they found huge footprints in the snow.

Howard-Bury reported what they saw to his base in India in a telegram. He either misunderstood or wrote incorrectly the word the Sherpas used for these creatures. Anyway, when it was translated into English, it came out "Abominable Snowman." "Abominable" means disgusting and disagreeable, but no one has ever gotten close enough to a Yeti to find out if that's what they really are.

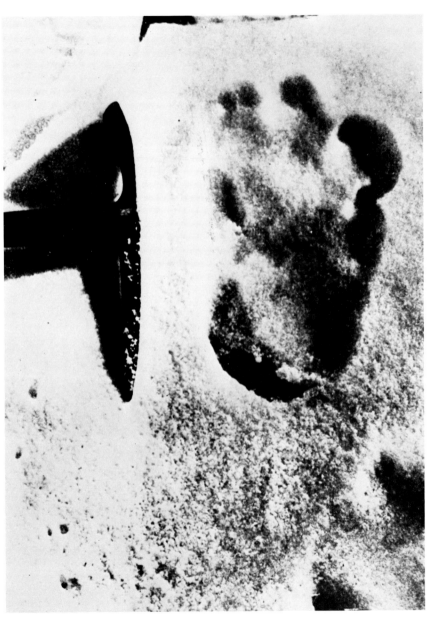

Shipton's photograph of a Yeti footprint (courtesy of THE BETTMANN AR-CHIVE)

And the Yeti are certainly not snowmen, at least not as we think of them. But the name is so catchy, it has been used ever since.

If You Don't Watch Out!

The Sherpas tell many stories of these fearsome, savage beasts that prowl by night and leave behind monstrous tracks in the snow. They say the beasts have high-pitched, whistling screams and a strong, terrible odor.

These people believe that if you see the Yeti, you will have bad luck or even die. They think that just hearing their eerie cry will bring on sickness. And their advice is, "If a Yeti chases you, run downhill. Its long hair will fall over its eyes and it won't be able to see you." Mothers warn their children, "The Yeti will get you if you aren't good."

Telltale Footprints

Many expeditions have traveled over the Himalayas in search of the Abominable Snowman. They have often found footprints, but people who deliberately look for the Yeti never seem to find them.

In 1951 British explorers Eric Shipton and Dr. Michael Ward saw some giant footprints on the Menlung Glacier. The prints were thirteen to eighteen inches long. The excited explorers followed the set of tracks until they disappeared on the hard ice. Whatever had made the giant prints was gone, but the prints were still there, and Shipton took photographs of them. The photographs were excellent. And it was clear that the footprints had not been

made by a bear, a monkey, a leopard, or a human being. Shipton said that although he had seen some tracks and heard many stories of the Yeti, he could not believe that the creatures existed. But when he found those tracks, made by naked feet, he knew that some large creature walked ahead of them on the glacier—and that it was not a human being or a known animal.

In Search of the Yeti

One of the most famous expeditions was led by Sir Edmund Hillary, the conqueror of Mount Everest. He and Tensing Norgay, his Sherpa guide, had found giant footprints while climbing to the top of Mount Everest in 1953.

Norgay, who was familiar with the Yeti stories, was sure they were Yeti footprints. Hillary was so interested that in 1960 he led a large expedition into the Himalayas in search of the Yeti.

Hillary and his men hoped they could prove that the Yeti really did exist. They set up cameras hoping to catch the creature on film, but the photographs never showed any mysterious creatures. One day the Sherpas did find some fresh tracks in the snow, but by the time the explorers got there, the sun had melted them. Though they searched and searched, Hillary and his men never found any evidence of the Yeti.

Hillary was allowed to bring back to England a dried

scalp, which the Sherpas said was a Yeti scalp. But the scientists who examined it quickly decided it was just the skin of a goat. After all this, Hillary decided that the whole idea of the Yeti was just a bunch of nonsense.

The Search Goes On

Others, though, have continued to believe and to look for the Yeti in the Himalayan Mountains. Recent expeditions have occasionally found footprints of a large, heavy creature that walks on two legs. They have sometimes caught a glimpse of a very tall, hairy creature in the distance. One expedition even found out that the Yeti like chocolate.

One night while camping in the Himalayas in 1977, Peter Boardman and Joe Tasker heard a growling creature searching through their supplies. They weren't sure what kind of animal might be out there, so they decided they had better stay hidden in their tents until it was light, then they could investigate.

What they found the next morning really surprised them. The creature ignored all the food in the camp except a box of chocolate bars. It took the chocolate—and left behind twelve-inch footprints.

Yet, despite all the stories, the search for Yeti, like the search for Bigfoot, still hasn't been able to provide scientists with any hard evidence that such creatures exist. All we know for sure is that if there are such creatures as the Yeti, the silent, snow-covered Himalayas make a great place for them to hide.

Other Ape-men

The Alma

In the U.S.S.R. there are many different names given to the man-beasts that have been seen there. The most popular is the "Alma."

The stories about Almas sound similar to Bigfoot and Yeti stories. The creatures are large and hairy, walk on two legs, and are difficult to find. However, the Almas are said to be more like wild men than like beasts. Reports tell of Almas using tools and warming themselves by a fire. One village said Almas even helped them in the fields.

During World War II the Russian army reportedly captured an Alma, thinking it was a spy. A man called in to examine the creature described it as six feet tall with a broad chest. It was covered with dark brown hair, except on its face, and had dull, empty eyes. The man concluded it was a wild man, not a spy in disguise. However, he learned later that the creature was shot anyway.

No one has actually kept an Alma—alive or dead. And so, despite all the stories, scientists say it doesn't exist either.

The Yeh ren

In the forests and mountains of China, the many reports of man-beasts have convinced some that huge, hairy creatures live there. They call them the Yeh ren. Scientific expeditions in the mid-1970's found footprints and hair, and natives have reported seeing half-human, half-ape creatures. However, in 1977 a huge expedition of scien-

Russian researcher Igor Burtsev compares his foot to cast of Alma footprint
(copyright Rene Dahinden)

71

tists, photographers, and soldiers spent eight months searching the forests for hard evidence. Not one of the 110 people involved so much as saw a mysterious creature. That may be because it was so difficult to travel through the thick forest and up steep cliffs. Or it may be because the creatures aren't there.

Gong Yulan shows Chinese investigators where she saw a "wild man" (copyright Rene Dahinden)

The Yowie

In Australia there are huge areas of forest and mountain where few, if any, people have ever set foot. From these areas come stories of (you guessed it!) huge, hairy creatures that seem to be half-human and half-beast. These big, hairy monsters are called the Yowies.

The Yowies seem to be much like the North American Bigfoot. They average between eight and twelve feet tall, are covered with hair, except on the face and hands, and appear to be more curious than aggressive.

Yowie sightings sound a lot like Bigfoot sightings:

In 1894 a boy named Johnnie McWilliams said that as he walked along the road one day, he saw a "wild man" step from behind a tree about thirty yards from the road. The creature just stood and looked at Johnnie for a few seconds. Then it turned and ran toward the hills. Johnnie said that it looked like a big man covered with long hair.

In 1912 George Summerell saw what he first thought was a kangaroo, drinking from a creek. When he got a closer look, he saw it wasn't a kangaroo at all. It was a hairy creature that looked somehow human.

In 1924 David Squires went on a kangaroo shoot. Suddenly he had the feeling he was not alone. Chills ran up and down his spine. When he turned around, he saw a creature about eight feet tall, standing beside a tree. It had greyish hair, grey-blue eyes, and a half-human, half-ape face! It watched Squires awhile and then walked away.

There have been many brief sightings such as these. But once again, no one has been able to show an actual Yowie to the scientists.

The Skunk Ape

From the swampy areas of Florida, Louisiana, and Texas come reports of huge, hairy creatures called skunk apes. These creatures may be Bigfoot which have wandered down from the Pacific Northwest, or they may be related animals. Whatever they are, they have a truly terrible odor, much like that of a skunk.

The skunk ape was brought to national attention in 1973, when a Florida man said his car hit a creature while it was crossing the road. The creature was hurt, but managed to limp off the road and into the dense swamp where it disappeared.

When the police examined the man's car, they found the fender dented and blood and fur on the car. A terrible smell hung in the air.

Others had reported the skunk ape before, but people had not paid much attention to them. Ralph "Bud" Chambers had reported one near his home in Elfers, Florida. He had noticed a terrible, sickening smell. Then he saw a big, hairy creature over seven feet tall and four feet wide. The huge, hairy thing vanished into the nearby swamp.

Chambers tried to track it, but his dogs were so bothered by the smell that they wouldn't follow the trail. A year later Chambers saw another one, this time in his backyard. His dogs attacked it, he said, but it just turned and walked away.

H.C. Osborn, an engineer and amateur archaelogist, said he never believed the skunk ape stories until one day when he and four friends were on an archaelogical dig in the Big Cypress Swamp in Florida. Suddenly a huge creature appeared right in front of them! It was seven feet tall, said Osborn, and weighed about 700 pounds. The footprints it left in the soft earth measured seventeen and one-half inches long and eleven and one-fourth inches across at the toes. "It made a believer out of me!" said Osborn.

In 1977 three boys told the Sheriff's Department of Charlotte County in Florida that they had seen the skunk ape twice in one night. Deputy Carl Williams drove to the spot where the boys said it had been. As Williams' headlights illuminated a small pond, Williams was amazed to see a large animal with brownish-red hair hunched over the pond. The animal seemed to be drinking the water. Williams studied the creature for a minute, wondering what it was. Before he could decide, the creature stood up and walked off into the woods.

"I'll believe the Yeti exist when one comes up and taps me on my shoulder!"

And There Are More

It seems that in every area of the world where people are few and forests are thick, there are stories about half-human, half-animal creatures. In addition to the stories described in this chapter, there are stories from Central America, South America, Africa, and even Japan. The scientists don't think there really are such creatures. They think somebody would have caught and kept one by now if they really existed. But the people who have seen these creatures declare that their stories are true. They say they know what they have seen, even if science can't explain it. What do you think?

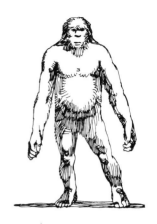

Chapter 5

Into the Supernatural

Super Bigfoot

Most scientists do not believe in the existence of Big-foot. But there are a few who admit there is a possibility that there is some unknown creature living in remote parts of the world. They think large, hairy animals which are unknown to science could hide in isolated parts of the world. But they believe that, if the Bigfoot exist, they are just that—unknown animals.

There are, though, people who claim the Bigfoot are not just animals. They claim the reason Bigfoot are never captured is because they can't be captured. They claim the Bigfoot have special powers. They claim the Bigfoot are supernatural!

Now You See It, Now You Don't

In Uniontown, Pennsylvania, a woman was disturbed one evening by cans rattling in front of her house. Thinking dogs had gotten into her garbage, she grabbed her shotgun and went outside to frighten them away. The woman, however, was the one to become frightened. A huge, hairy, ape-like creature stood just a few feet away. Without thinking, the woman fired at the creature point-blank. But the bullet never hit the creature because the creature disappeared in a flash of light.

This story and others like it tell of creatures which have incredible ability to vanish into thin air. People have reported Bigfoot walking through gooey mud and not leaving any footprints or moving through thick bushes and not making a sound. Some have seen a huge, hairy creature and claimed that they were able to see right through it. Perhaps the Bigfoot have a lot in common with ghosts!

Faster Than a Speeding Bullet

And there are those who say a Bigfoot can never be killed. No matter how many bullets you fire at it, you'll never even injure it.

In 1977 a farmer in New Jersey fired three or four times at a Bigfoot with a gun he used for deer hunting. The farmer was sure he hit the creature, but the creature's only reaction was to growl.

In 1980 a family watching television in their Kentucky home was disturbed by something rattling their back door. It sounded like someone trying to get in. When one

of the members of the family went to investigate, he saw a seven-foot tall, white-haired Bigfoot. The man fired two pistol shots at it, but the creature just walked away, unaffected by the bullets.

Some say the stories about Bigfoot being unaffected by bullets could be true. But that wouldn't necessarily mean the Bigfoot have supernatural powers. If the light were dim and the people were scared, they might have thought they hit the creature, but actually they didn't. Also a creature as large as Bigfoot might not be affected immediately by a small bullet. It takes a special kind of gun to shoot an elephant or hippopotamus or any very large animal. The Bigfoot might be hit and still be able to run away. Later it might feel the effect of the bullet. Others say even that would prove the Bigfoot are not ordinary.

UFOs

Stories of animals that vanish or can't be hit by bullets are strange enough, but the weirdest reports of all link Bigfoot with UFOs. Now that seems a very odd combination—a big, hairy monster out of the past and something from the most modern science fiction. However, there have been many stories of Bigfoot sightings occuring at the same time as UFO sightings.

One August night in 1973, a man in Roachdale, Indiana, said that he saw a shining object in the sky over a cornfield. Later that night the family heard noises out in the yard. One of the men went out to see what was happening. He saw a large, broad-shouldered creature heading for the cornfield.

On other nights the family said they saw the creature again. It was covered with black hair and smelled terrible —like garbage or a dead animal! The creature was weird, said the family, and very mysterious. Sometimes they could see right through it. And when it ran through the weeds, they couldn't hear a sound!

Neighbors saw the monster. It killed their chickens and stole their vegetables. They chased it and shot at it, but

the creature was not harmed. After a while it was no longer seen there, but reports of it came from farther north.

In 1973 near Uniontown, Pennsylvania, some people said that they saw a red ball in the sky and then a bright, white object in a pasture. Those who walked out to see what it was said they saw two, tall, ape-like creatures with glowing green eyes, walking around in the woods. After the creatures and the UFO were gone, there was a smell of sulfur in the air, and the people in the area felt light-headed and short-of-breath.

One of the most famous Bigfoot/UFO encounters happened in July of 1966.

Six people were on a picnic near Erie, Pennsylvania. Their car got stuck, and one man went for help. While the others waited, they saw a bright light move through the

night sky and "land" on the beach. The people could see a mushroom-shaped craft with three lights. It was now about ten o'clock at night, and the lights from the craft lit up the whole area.

A police car approached to help with the stuck car. The lights on the UFO went out, but the picnickers quickly told the police officer what they had seen. The police officer and one of the car's occupants went to investigate. They hadn't gone far, though, before they heard the car horn blaring.

The two men hurried back to the car and found the people there terrified. A large, dark creature had approached the car and scratched at the sides and roof.

Everyone was now more scared than curious, so they left. The next day, though, two police officers found marks in the ground where the UFO had landed and

"Bigfoot?! Next you'll be wanting me to believe in UFOs!"

tracks leading from that spot to where the car had been. The tracks were round and seemed to have claws. Also, the people whose car had been stuck found that there was a dent in their car roof which had not been there before.

What to Believe?

Those that believe there is a link between Bigfoot and UFOs are not sure whether the Bigfoot are alien creatures coming from some other planet or if aliens are "borrowing" our Bigfoot and experimenting on them. Most people, however, doubt there is any connection between Bigfoot and UFOs. They seem simply to be two unsolved puzzles that get linked together because they are so mysterious.

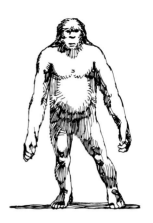

Chapter 6
What is Bigfoot?

Whatever Bigfoot is or isn't remains a mystery. Every year there are hundreds of sightings of the creature or its footprints. Yet we never seem to get any closer to the truth. There remain many possibilities for what Bigfoot might be.

A Hoax

There is always the possibility that the whole Bigfoot mystery is the result of hoaxes. Most scientists think this is the case, and so do many other people.

There is no doubt that many people have just pretended to see Bigfoot. They might have wanted their names in the paper, or they might have liked the idea of fooling people. However, this doesn't explain the sincere people who have reported something that genuinely puzzled or scared them. Over and over again, investigators have interviewed witnesses who had no reason for lying, witnesses with excellent reputations and good powers of observation.

These people may have been fooled by other people dressing up in gorilla suits. There have been those who have done this because they think it is fun to fool Bigfoot hunters or scare tourists. Some of the photographs that have been taken have been shown to be this kind of fake. And if some of them are fakes, maybe all of them are.

However, many believers in Bigfoot argue that most sightings could not possibly be dismissed as just a man in a monkey suit. The creature seen is too large or can do things no human can do. And, say the believers, people would have to be crazy to dress up—too many people have taken a shot at Bigfoot!

Footprints, too, have been found to be faked. People have cut old tires or pieces of wood into the shape of huge feet and then walked around making prints. Experts can usually recognize these kinds of fakes fairly easily. They aren't deep enough for the heavy creature, or they aren't the shape of a real foot. There are footprints that have withstood the closest analysis, but there is always the chance that they are just well-done fakes.

Mistaken Identity

Often, sincere people have seen stumps or clumps of bushes and thought they were seeing a real, live Bigfoot. A case of mistaken identity can easily happen in a lonely spot at night—especially if a person has monsters on his

Dennis Gates poses in a fur suit used in a Bigfoot hoax (copyright Rene Dahinden)

mind. Also, bears and other wild animals can be mistaken for Bigfoot if glimpsed only briefly.

Footprints, too, may be misunderstood. If an animal walks so that its back feet overlap the prints left by its front feet, it can leave behind large, unusual prints. Or, snow can melt around the edge of a print, making it appear much larger than it really is. However, experts can usually tell if these things have really happened.

An Unknown Animal

There is, though, the possibility that the Bigfoot do exist. If they do, they might be animals that have not yet been identified—some unknown species, even an endangered species.

There have been other animals that have surprised the experts. Scientists once thought that all the fish of a kind called the coelacanth had been dead for years. Then one was discovered off the coast of Africa. Until 1870 a giant squid called the kraken was thought to be only a myth. Fishermen kept reporting seeing them, but the scientists didn't believe them—until one was brought in. The Giant Panda wasn't discovered until 1869. And the white rhino was discovered in Africa in 1910.

Bigfoot might be another unknown species not yet discovered and classified by scientists.

A Giant Ape

If the Bigfoot are animals, what kind of animal might they be? Scientists have suggested a few possibilities.

Bigfoot might be descended from a line of gigantic apes

Is Bigfoot related to the ape? (copyright Rene Dahinden)

that lived in south central and southeast Asia 500,000 years ago. Scientists have found the remains of a creature that seemed to be half-ape and half-human. It seems hard to believe that such creatures could have survived from that long ago without anyone knowing of them, but who knows?

Some scientists, though, think that if there are Bigfoot, they are more likely to be related to the orangutans. Many witnesses to Bigfoot sightings have selected pictures of the orangutan as being the closest to what they saw.

Wild Man

Others think Bigfoot is more human than animal. They think Bigfoot might have descended from prehistoric man. Now, a Bigfoot can't be just a person who decided to go off and live in the woods by himself who became "wild." Living alone in the woods doesn't make a person suddenly grow hair all over his body and grow a foot or two taller. But some people believe there could have been a tribe or two of prehistoric people that survived the Ice Age and lived on, isolated from all other people. They could have many of the characteristics Bigfoot is said to have.

No Place to Hide

Some people say if there were Bigfoot, we would see more of them. There aren't many hiding places left, they say, in this land of towns and cities and suburban areas. But the truth is there are thousands of square miles of wilderness—mountains, forests, and valleys where no one lives and few people go exploring—especially in the Pacific Northwest. And in the rest of the world, there are still many, many areas that are uninhabited and unexplored.

Where Are the Skeletons?

Another question people ask is: if the Bigfoot exist, why has no one ever found any skeletons, skulls, or bones? Here, too, there are some possible answers. Maybe the Bigfoot bury their dead. Maybe their bones disintegrate. In wet, acid soil, bones do not turn into fossils but just gradually disappear.

Maybe the "clean-up crews," the garbage disposals of the forests—buzzards, crows, coyotes, and black bears— eat the dead animals. Few people have ever found the

bones of a dead bear or mountain lion, so maybe we should not expect to find any of Bigfoot.

What is the Answer?

Is Bigfoot out there? Is it possible or even probable that such creatures exist? This riddle may never be solved—and maybe we don't want it to be. Sometimes "maybe" is more exciting than "for sure." Sometimes playing the "are they or aren't they" game is more fun than actually knowing.

Is Bigfoot out there—lurking in the forests, peeking at us from behind tall trees, playing the game of hide-and-seek?

That's the Great Mystery!

INDEX